ALSO BY HARUKI MURAKAMI

FICTION

1Q84
After Dark
After the Quake
Blind Willow, Sleeping Woman
The City and Its Uncertain Walls
Colorless Tsukuru Tazaki and His Years of Pilgrimage
Dance Dance Dance
The Elephant Vanishes
First Person Singular
Hard-Boiled Wonderland and the End of the World
Kafka on the Shore
Killing Commendatore
Men Without Women
Norwegian Wood
South of the Border, West of the Sun
Sputnik Sweetheart
The Strange Library
A Wild Sheep Chase
Wind/Pinball
The Wind-Up Bird Chronicle

NON-FICTION

Absolutely on Music: Conversations with Seiji Ozawa
Novelist as a Vocation
Underground: The Tokyo Gas Attack and the Japanese Psyche
What I Talk About When I Talk About Running: A Memoir
Murakami T: The T-Shirts I Love

Super-Frog Saves Tokyo
HARUKI MURAKAMI

Translated from the Japanese
by Jay Rubin

HARVILL

LONDON

5 7 9 10 8 6 4

Harvill, an imprint of Vintage, is part of the
Penguin Random House group of companies

Vintage, Penguin Random House UK, One Embassy Gardens,
8 Viaduct Gardens, London SW11 7BW

penguin.co.uk/vintage
global.penguinrandomhouse.com

This edition first published by Harvill in 2025
The story 'Super-Frog Saves Tokyo' first appeared in *GQ* in 2001
First published in Great Britain in *after the quake* by The Harvill Press in 2002
Originally published in *Kami no kodomo-tachi wa mina odoru* in Japan,
by Shinchosha Publishing Co., Ltd, Tokyo in 2000

Copyright © Harukimurakami Archival Labyrinth 2000

The moral right of the author has been asserted

Translated from the Japanese by Jay Rubin with the participation of the author

Design © Suzanne Dean

Penguin Random House values and supports copyright. Copyright fuels creativity,
encourages diverse voices, promotes freedom of expression and supports a vibrant culture.
Thank you for purchasing an authorised edition of this book and for respecting intellectual
property laws by not reproducing, scanning or distributing any part of it by any means
without permission. You are supporting authors and enabling Penguin Random House to
continue to publish books for everyone. No part of this book may be used or reproduced in
any manner for the purpose of training artificial intelligence technologies or systems.
In accordance with Article 4(3) of the DSM Directive 2019/790, Penguin Random House
expressly reserves this work from the text and data mining exception.

Printed and bound in Italy by L.E.G.O. S.p.A.

The authorised representative in the EEA is Penguin Random House Ireland,
Morrison Chambers, 32 Nassau Street, Dublin D02 YH68

A CIP catalogue record for this book is available from the British Library

ISBN 9781787304710

Penguin Random House is committed to a sustainable future for our business, our readers
and our planet. This book is made from Forest Stewardship Council® certified paper.

Katagiri found a giant frog waiting for him in his apartment.

It was powerfully built, standing over six feet tall on its hind legs. A skinny little man no more than five foot three, Katagiri was overwhelmed by the frog's imposing bulk.

"**Call me 'Frog,'**" said the frog in a clear, strong voice.

ぼくのことはかえるくんと呼んで下さい

Katagiri stood rooted in the doorway, unable to speak.

"Don't be afraid. I'm not here to hurt you. Just come and close the door. Please."

Briefcase in his right hand, grocery bag with fresh vegetables and canned salmon cradled in his left arm, Katagiri didn't dare move.

"Please, Mr. Katagiri, hurry and close the door, and take off your shoes."

The sound of his own name helped Katagiri to snap out of it. He closed the door as ordered, set the grocery bag on the raised wooden floor, pinned the briefcase under one arm and untied his shoes. Frog gestured for him to take a seat at the kitchen table, which he did.

"I must apologize, Mr. Katagiri, for having barged in while you were out," Frog said. "I knew it would be a shock for you to find me here. I but had no choice. How about a cup of tea? I thought you would be coming home soon, so I boiled some water."

Katagiri still had his briefcase jammed under his arm. Somebody's playing a joke on me, he thought. Somebody's rigged himself up in this huge frog costume just to have fun with me. But he knew, as he watched Frog pour boiling water into the teapot, humming all the while, that these had to be the limbs and movements of a real frog. Frog set a cup of green tea in front of Katagiri and poured another one for himself.

Sipping his tea, Frog asked, "Calming down?"

答えはイエノーです。

But still Katagiri could not speak.

"I know I should have made an appointment to visit you, Mr. Katagiri. I am fully aware of the proprieties. Anyone would be shocked to find a big frog waiting for him at home. But an urgent matter brings me here. Please forgive me."

"Urgent matter?" Katagiri managed to produce words at last.

"Yes, indeed," Frog said. "Why else would I take the liberty of barging into a person's home? Such discourtesy is not my customary style."

"Does this 'matter' have something to do with me?"

"**Yes and no,**" Frog said with a tilt of the head. "**No and yes.**"

ノーであり、

スであり、

イエスです。

I've got to get a grip on myself, thought Katagiri. "Do you mind if I smoke?"

"Not at all, not at all," Frog said with a smile. "It's your home. You don't have to ask my permission. Smoke and drink as much as you like. I myself am not a smoker, but I can hardly impose my distaste for tobacco on others in their own homes.

Katagiri pulled a pack of cigarettes from his coat pocket and struck a match. He saw his hand trembling as he lit up. Seated opposite him, Frog seemed to be studying his every movement.

"You don't happen to be connected with some kind of gang by any chance?" Katagiri found the courage to ask.

"Ha ha ha ha ha ha! What a wonderful sense of humor you have, Mr. Katagiri!" Frog said, slapping his webbed hand against his thigh. "There may be a shortage of skilled labor, but what

gang is going to hire a frog to do their dirty work? They'd be made a laughing stock."

"Well, if you're here to negotiate a repayment, you're wasting your time. I have no authority to make such decisions. Only my superiors can do that, I just follow orders. I can't do a thing for you."

"Please, Mr. Katagiri," Frog said, raising one webbed finger. "I have not come here on such petty business. I am fully aware that you are Assistant Chief of the lending division of the Shinjuku branch of the Tokyo Security Trust Bank. But my visit has nothing to do with the repayment of loans. I have come here to save Tokyo from destruction."

Katagiri scanned the room for a hidden TV camera in case he was being made the butt of some huge, terrible joke. But there was no camera. It was a small apartment. There was no place for anyone to hide.

"No," Frog said. "We are the only ones here. I know you are thinking that I must be mad or that you are having some kind of dream, but I am not crazy and you are not dreaming. This is absolutely, positively serious."

"To tell you the truth, Mr. Frog—"

"Please," Frog said, raising one finger again. "Call me 'Frog.'"

"To tell you the truth, Frog," Katagiri said, "I can't quite understand what is going on here. It's not that I don't trust you, but I don't seem to be able to grasp the situation exactly. Do you mind if I ask you a question or two?"

"Not at all, not at all," Frog said. "Mutual understanding is of critical importance. There are those who say that 'understanding' is merely the sum total of our misunderstandings, and while I do find this view interesting in its own way, I am afraid we have no time to spare on pleasant digressions. The best thing would be for us to achieve mutual understanding via the shortest possible route. Therefore, by all means, ask as many questions as you wish."

げええ

"Now; you are a real frog, am I right?"

"Yes, of course, as you can see. A real frog is exactly what I am. A product neither of metaphor nor allusion nor deconstruction nor sampling nor any other such complex process, I am a genuine frog. Shall I croak for you?"

えええ

お、う

こ、うぐ
えええ
えこお

Frog tilted back his head and flexed the muscles of his huge throat. Ribit. Ri-i-i-bit. Ribit ribit ribit. Ribit. Ribit. Ri-i-i bit. His gigantic croaks rattled the pictures hanging on the walls.

ぐっく。

"Fine, I see, I see!" Katagiri said, worried about the thin walls of the cheap apartment house in which he lived. "That's great. You are, without question, a real frog."

"One might also say that I am the sum total of all frogs. Nonetheless, this does nothing to change the fact that I am a frog. Anyone claiming that I am not a frog would be a dirty liar. I would smash such a person to bits!"

Katagiri nodded. Hoping to calm himself, he picked up his cup and swallowed a mouthful of tea. "You said before that you have come here to save Tokyo from destruction?"

"That is what I said."

"What kind of destruction?"

"Earthquake," Frog said with the utmost gravity.

Mouth dropping open, Katagiri looked at Frog. And Frog, saying nothing, looked at Katagiri. They went on staring at each other like this for some time. Next it was Frog's turn to open his mouth.

"A very, very big earthquake. It is set to strike Tokyo at 8:30 a.m. on February 18. Three days from now. A much bigger earthquake than the one that struck Kobe last month. The number of dead from such a quake would probably exceed 150,000—mostly from accidents involving the commuter system: derailments, falling vehicles, crashes, the collapse of elevated expressways and rail lines, the crushing of subways, the explosion of tanker trucks. Buildings will be transformed into piles of rubble, their inhabitants crushed to death. Fires everywhere, the road system in a state of collapse, ambulances and fire trucks useless, people just lying there, dying. One hundred and fifty thousand of them! Pure hell. People will be made to realize what a fragile condition the intensive collectivity known as 'city' really is." Frog said this with a gentle shake of the bead. "The epicenter will be close to the Shinjuku ward office."

"Close to the Shinjuku ward office?"

"To be precise, it will hit directly beneath the Shinjuku branch of the Tokyo Security Trust Bank."

A heavy silence followed.

重い沈黙が続いた。

"Exactly," Frog said, nodding. "That is exactly what I propose to do. You and I will go underground beneath the Shinjuku branch of the Tokyo Security Trust Bank to do mortal combat with Worm."

As a member of the Trust Bank lending division, Katagiri had fought his way through many a battle. He had weathered sixteen years of daily combat since the day he graduated from the university and joined the bank's staff. He was, in a word, a collection officer—a post that won him little popularity. Everyone in his division preferred to make loans, especially at the time of the bubble. They had so much money in those days that almost any likely piece of collateral—be it land or stock—was enough to convince loan officers to give away whatever they were asked for, the bigger the loan the better their reputations in the company. Some loans, though, never made it back to the bank: They got "stuck to the bottom of the pan." It was Katagiri's job to take care of those. And when the bubble burst, the work piled on. First stock prices fell, and then land values, and collateral lost all significance. "Get out there," his boss commanded him, "and squeeze whatever you can out of them."

The Kabukicho neighborhood of Shinjuku was a labyrinth of violence: old-time gangsters, Korean mobsters, Chinese Mafia, guns and drugs, money flowing beneath the surface from one murky den to another, people vanishing every now and then like puffs of smoke. Plunging into Kabukicho to collect a bad debt, Katagiri had been surrounded more than once by mobsters threatening to kill him, but he had never been frightened.

What good would it have done them to kill one man running around for the bank? They could stab him if they wanted to. They could beat him up. He was perfect for the job: no wife, no kids, both parents dead, a brother and sister he had put through college married off. So what if they killed him? It wouldn't change anything for anybody—least of all for Katagiri himself.

It was not Katagiri but the thugs surrounding him who got nervous when they saw him so calm and cool. He soon earned a kind of reputation in their world as a tough guy. Now, though, the tough Katagiri was at a total loss. What the hell was this frog talking about?

"Worm lives underground. He is a gigantic worm. When he gets angry, he causes **earthquakes**," Frog said. "And right now he is very, very angry."

"What is he angry about?" Katagiri asked.

"I have no idea," Frog said. "Nobody knows what Worm is thinking inside that murky head of his. Few have ever seen him. He is usually asleep. That's what he really likes to do: take long, long naps. He goes on sleeping for years—decades—in the warmth and darkness underground. His eyes, as you might imagine, have atrophied, his brain has turned to jelly as he sleeps. If you ask me, I'd guess he probably isn't thinking anything at all, just lying there and feeling every little rumble and reverberation that comes his way, absorbing them into his body and storing them up. And then, through some kind of chemical process, he replaces most of them with rage. Why this happens I have no idea. I could never explain it."

Frog fell silent watching Katagiri and waiting until his words had sunk in. Then

he went on: "Please don't misunderstand me, though. I feel no personal animosity toward Worm. I don't see him as the embodiment of evil. Not that I would want to be his friend, either: I just think that as far as the world is concerned, it is, in a sense, all right for a being like him to exist. The world is like a great big overcoat, and it needs pockets of various shapes and sizes. But right at the moment, Worm has reached the point where he is too dangerous to ignore. With all the different kinds of hatred he has absorbed and stored inside himself over the years, his heart and body have swollen to gargantuan proportions—bigger than ever before. And to make matters worse, last month's Kobe earthquake shook him out of the deep sleep he was enjoying. He experienced a revelation inspired by his profound rage: It was time now for him, too, to cause a massive earthquake, and he'd do it here, in Tokyo.

"I know what I'm talking about, Mr. Katagiri: I have received reliable information on the timing and scale of the earthquake from some of my best bug friends."

Frog snapped his mouth shut and closed his round eyes in apparent fatigue.

"So what you're saying is," Katagiri said, "that you and I have to go underground together and fight Worm to stop the earthquake."

"Exactly."

Katagiri reached for his cup of tea, picked it up and put it back. "I still don't get it," he said. "Why did you choose me to go with you?"

Frog looked straight into Katagiri's eyes and said "I have always had the profoundest respect for you, Mr. Katagiri. For sixteen long years, you have silently accepted the most dangerous, least glamorous assignments—the jobs that others have avoided—and you have carried them off beautifully. I know full well how difficult this has been for you, and I do not believe that either your superiors or your colleagues properly appreciate your accomplishments. They are blind, the whole lot of them. But you, unappreciated and unpromoted, have never once complained.

"Nor is it simply a matter of your work. After your parents died, you raised your teenage brother and sister single-handedly, put them through college and even arranged for them to marry, all at great sacrifice of your time and income, and at the expense of your own marriage prospects. In spite of this, your brother and sister have never once expressed gratitude for your efforts on their behalf. Far from it. They have shown you no respect and acted with the most callous disregard for your loving kindness. In my opinion, their behavior is unconscionable. I almost wish I could beat them to a pulp on your behalf. But you, meanwhile, show no trace of anger.

"To be quite honest, Mr. Katagiri, you are nothing much to look at, and you are far from eloquent, so you tend to be looked down upon by those around you. I, however, can see what a sensible and courageous man you are. In all of Tokyo, with its teeming millions, there is no one else I could trust as much as you to fight by my side."

"Tell me, Mr. Frog," Katagiri said.

"Please," Frog said, raising one finger again. "Call me 'Frog.'"

"Tell me, Frog," Katagiri said, "how do you know so much about me?"

"Well, Mr. Katagiri, I have not been frogging all these years for nothing. I keep my eye on the important things in life."

"But still, Frog," Katagiri said. "I'm not particularly strong, and I don't know anything about what's happening underground. I don't have the kind of muscle it will take to fight Worm in the darkness. I'm sure you can find somebody a lot stronger than me—a man who does karate, say, or a Self-Defense Forces commando."

Frog rolled his large eyes. "Tell you the truth, Mr. Katagiri," he said, "I'm the one who will do all the fighting. But I can't do it alone. This is the key thing: I need your courage and your passion for justice. I need you to stand behind me and say, 'Way to go, Frog! You're doing great! I know you can win! You're fighting the good fight!'"

Frog opened his arms wide, then slapped his webbed hands down on his knees again.

"In all honesty, Mr. Katagiri, the thought of fighting Worm in the dark frightens me, too. For many years I lived as a pacifist, loving art, living with nature. Fighting is not something I like to do. I do it because I have to. And this particular fight will be a fierce one; that is certain. I may not return from it alive. I may lose a limb or two in the process. But I cannot— I will not—run away. As Nietzsche said, the highest wisdom is

to have no fear. What I want from you, Mr. Katagiri, is for you to share your simple courage with me, to support me with your whole heart as a true friend. Do you understand what I am trying to tell you?"

None of this made any sense to Katagiri, but still he felt that—unreal as it sounded—he could believe whatever Frog said to him. Something about Frog—the look on his face, the way he spoke—had a simple honesty that appealed directly to the heart. After years of work in the toughest division of the Security Trust Bank, Katagiri possessed the ability to sense such things. It was all but second nature to him.

"I know this must be difficult for you, Mr. Katagiri. A huge frog comes barging into your place and asks you to believe all these outlandish things. Your reaction is perfectly natural. And so I intend to provide you with proof that I exist. Tell me, Mr. Katagiri: you have been having a great deal of trouble
recovering a loan the bank

made to Big Bear Trading, have you not?"

"That's true," Katagiri said.

"Well, they have a number of extortionist working behind the scenes, and those individuals are mixed up with the mobsters. They're scheming to make the company go bankrupt and get out of its debts. Your bank's loan officer shoved a pile of cash at them without a decent background check, and, as usual, the one who's left to clean up after him is you, Mr. Katagiri. But you're having a hard times sinking your teeth into these fellows: They're no push-overs. And there may be a powerful politician backing them up. They're into you for 700 million. That is the situation you are dealing with, am I right?"

"You certainly are."

Frog stretched his arms out wide, his big green webs opening like pale wings.

"Don't worry, Mr. Katagiri. Leave everything to me. By tomorrow morning, old Frog will have your problems solved. Relax and have a good night's sleep."

With a big smile on his face, Frog stood up. Then, flattening himself like a dried squid, he slipped out through the gap at the side of the closed door, leaving Katagiri all alone. The two teacups on the kitchen table were the only indication that Frog had ever been in Katagiri's apartment.

◉ ◉ ◉ ◉ ◉ ◉ ◉ ◉

The moment Katagiri arrived at work the next morning at nine, the phone on his desk rang.

"Mr. Katagiri," said a man's voice. It was cold and business-like. "My name is Shiraoka. I'm an attorney with the Big Bear case. I received a call from my client this morning with regard to the pending loan matter. He wants you to know that he will take full responsibility for returning the entire amount requested, by the due date. He will also give you a signed memorandum to that effect. His only request is that you do not send Frog to his home again. I repeat: He wants you to ask Frog never to visit his home again. I'm not entirely sure what this is supposed to mean, but I believe it should be clear to you, Mr. Katagiri. Am I correct?"

"You are indeed," Katagiri said.

"You will be kind enough to convey my message to Frog, I trust."

"That I will do. Your client will never see Frog again."

"Thank you very much. I will prepare the memorandum for you by tomorrow."

"I appreciate it," Katagiri said.

The connection was cut.

Frog visited Katagiri in his Trust Bank office at lunchtime. "I assume that Big Bear case is working out well for you?"

Katagiri glanced around uneasily.

"Don't worry," Frog said. "You are the only one who can see me. But now I am sure you realize I actually exist. I am not a product of your imagination. I can take action and produce results. I am a living being."

"Tell me, Mr. Frog," Katagiri said.

"Please," Frog said, raising one finger. "Call me '**Frog**.'"

"Tell me, Frog," Katagiri said. "What did you do to them?"

"Oh, nothing much," Frog said. "Nothing much more complicated than boiling Brussels sprouts. I just gave them a little scare. A touch of psychological terror. As Joseph Conrad once wrote, true terror is the kind that men feel toward their imagination. But never mind that, Mr. Katagiri. Tell me about the Big Bear case. It is working out well, I assume?"

Katagiri nodded and lit a cigarette. "Seems to be."

"So, then, have I succeeded in gaining your trust with regard to the matter I broached to you last night? Will you join me to fight against Worm?"

Sighing, Katagiri removed his glasses and wiped them. "To tell you the truth, I am not too crazy about the idea, but I don't suppose that's enough to get me out of it."

"No," Frog said. "It is a matter of responsibility and honor. You may not be '**too crazy**' about the idea, but we have no choice: You and I must go underground and face Worm. If we should happen to lose our lives in the process, we will gain no one's sympathy. And even if we manage to defeat Worm, no one will praise us. No one will ever know that such a battle even raged far beneath their feet. Only you and I will know, Mr. Katagiri. However it turns out, ours will be a lonely battle."

Katagiri looked at his own hand for a while, then watched the smoke rising from his cigarette. Finally, he spoke. "You know Mr. Frog, I'm just an ordinary person."

"Make that 'Frog,' please," Frog said, but Katagiri let it go.

「気が進」

"I'm an absolutely ordinary guy. Less than ordinary. I'm going bald, I'm getting a potbelly, I turned 40 last month. My feet are flat. The doctor told me recently that I have diabetic tendencies. It's been three months or more since I last slept with a woman—and I had to pay for it. I do get some recognition within the division for my ability to collect on loans, but no real respect. I don't have a single person who likes me, either at work or in my private life. I don't know how to talk to people, and I'm bad with strangers, so I never make friends. I have no athletic ability, I'm tone-deaf, short, phimotic, near sighted—and astigmatic. I live a horrible life. All I do is eat, sleep and shit. I don't know why I'm even living. Why should a person like me have to be the one to save Tokyo?"

"Because, Mr. Katagiri, Tokyo can only be saved by a person like you. And it's for people like you that I am trying to save Tokyo."

Katagiri sighed again, more deeply this time. "All right, then, what do you want me to do?"

Frog told Katagiri his plan. They would go underground on the night of February 17 (one day before the earthquake was scheduled to happen). Their way in would be through the basement boiler room of the Shinjuku branch of the Tokyo Security Trust Bank. They would meet there late at night (Katagiri would stay in the building on the pretext of working overtime). Behind a section of wall was a vertical shaft, and they would find Worm at the bottom by climbing down a 150-foot rope ladder.

"Do you have a battle plan in mind?" Katagiri asked.

"Of course I do. We would have no hope of defeating an enemy like Worm without a battle plan. He is a slimy creature: You can't tell his mouth from his anus. And he is as big as a commuter train."

"What is your battle plan?"

After a thoughtful pause Frog answered, "Hmm, what is it they say—'Silence is golden?'"

"You mean I shouldn't ask?"

"That's one way of putting it."

"What if I get scared at the last minute and run away? What would you do then, Mr. Frog?"

"'Frog.'"

"Frog. What would you do then?"

Л. Н. ТОЛСТОЙ

АННА
КАРЕНИНА

Frog thought about this awhile and answered, "I would fight on alone. My chances of beating him by myself are perhaps just slightly better than Anna Karenina's chances of beating that speeding locomotive. Have you read *Anna Karenina*, Mr. Katagiri?"

When he heard that Katagiri had not read the novel, Frog gave him a look as if to say "What a shame." Apparently, Frog was very fond of *Anna Karenina*.

"Still, Mr. Katagiri, I do not believe that you will leave me to fight alone. I can tell. It's a question of balls—which, unfortunately, I do not happen to possess. Ha ha ha ha." Frog laughed with his mouth wide open. Balls were not all that Frog lacked. He had no teeth either.

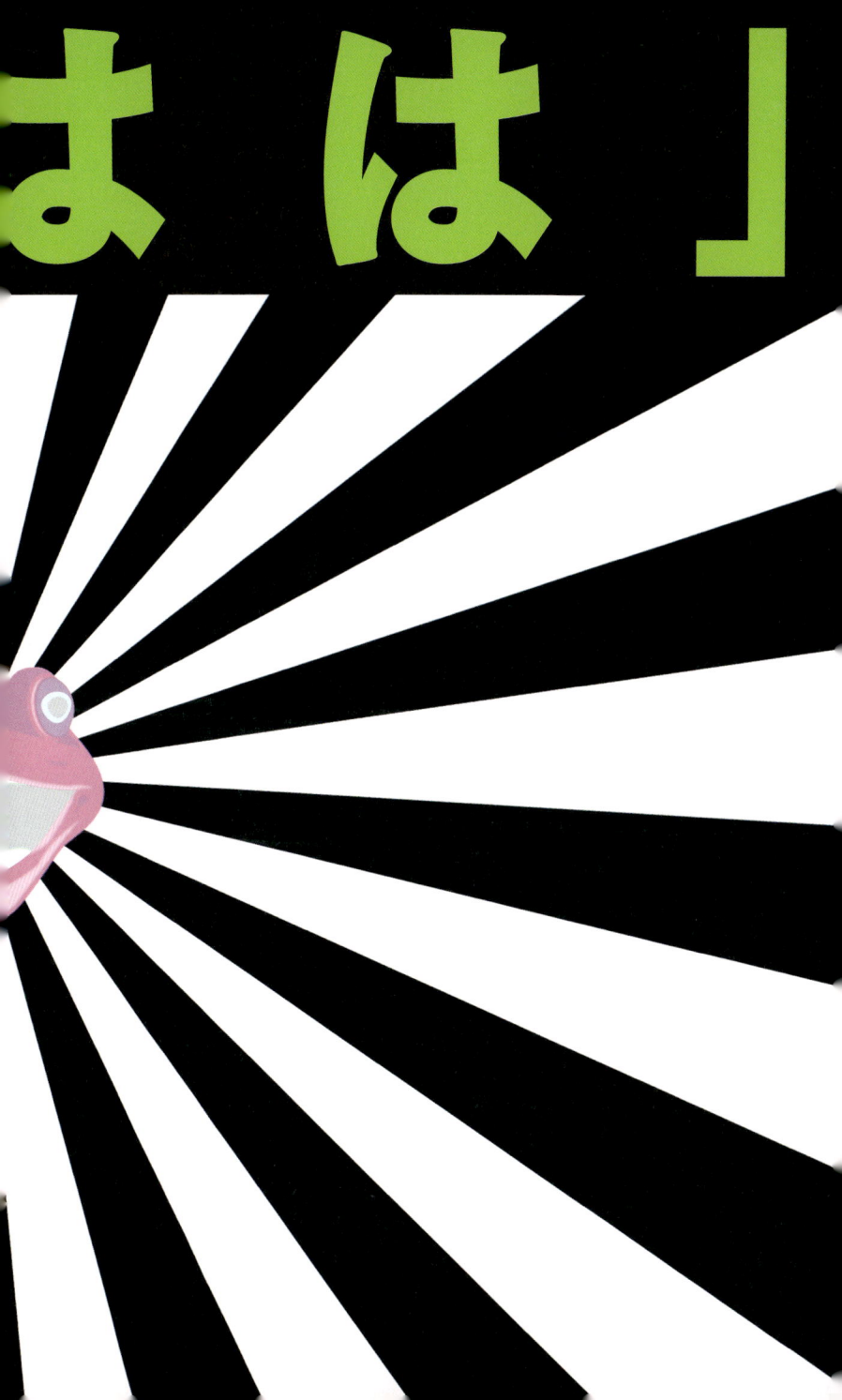

Unexpected things do happen, however.

Katagiri was shot on the evening of February 17. He had finished his rounds for the day and was walking down the street in Shinjuku on his way back to the Trust Bank when a young man in a leather jacket leaped in front of him. The man's face was a blank, and he gripped a small black gun in one hand. The gun was so small and so black that it hardly looked real. Katagiri stared at the object in the man's hand, not registering the fact that it was aimed at him and that the man was pulling the trigger. It all happened too quickly: It didn't make sense to him. But the gun, in fact, went off.

Katagiri saw the barrel jerk in the air and, at the same moment, felt an impact as though someone had struck his right shoulder with a sledgehammer. He felt no pain, but the blow sent him sprawling on the sidewalk. The leather briefcase in his right hand went flying in the other direction. The man aimed the gun at him again. A second shot rang out. A small eatery's sidewalk signboard exploded before his eyes. He heard people screaming. His glasses had flown off, and everything was a blur. He was vaguely aware that the man was approaching with the pistol pointed at him. I'm going to die, he thought. Frog had said that true terror is the kind men feel toward their imagination.

Katagiri cut the switch of his imagination and sank into a weightless silence.

when he woke up, he was in bed. He opened one eye, took a moment to survey his surroundings and then opened the other eye. The first thing that entered his field of vision was a metal stand by the head of the bed and an intravenous feeding tube that stretched from the stand to where he lay. Next he saw a nurse dressed in white. He realized he was lying on his back on a hard bed and wearing some strange piece of clothing under which he seemed to be naked.

Oh yeah, he thought, I was walking along the sidewalk when some guy shot me. Probably in the shoulder. The right one. He relived the scene in his mind. When he remembered the small black gun in the young man's hand, his heart made a disturbing thump. The sons of bitches were trying to kill me! he thought. But it looks as if I made it through OK. My memory is fine. I don't have any pain. And not just pain: I don't have any feeling at all. I can't lift my arm…

The hospital room had no windows. He could not tell whether it was day or night. He had been shot just before five in the evening. How much time had passed since then? Had the hour of his night time rendezvous with Frog gone by? Katagiri searched the room for a clock, but without his glasses he could see nothing at a distance.

"Excuse me," he called to the nurse.

"Oh, good. You're finally awake," the nurse said.

"What time is it?"

She glanced at her watch.

"Nine-fifteen."

"P.M.?"

"Don't be silly; it's morning!"

"Nine-fifteen a.m.?" Katagiri groaned, barely managing to lift his head from the pillow. The ragged noise that emerged from his throat sounded like someone else's voice. "Nine-fifteen a.m. on February 18?"

"Right," the nurse said, lifting her arm once more to check the date on her digital watch. "Today is February 18, 1995."

"Wasn't there a big earthquake in Tokyo this morning?"

"In Tokyo?"

"In Tokyo."

The nurse shook her head. "Not as far as I know."

He breathed a sigh of relief. Whatever had happened, the earthquake at least had been averted.

"How's my wound doing?"

"Your wound?" she asked. "What wound?"

"Where I was shot."

"Shot?"

"Yeah, near the entrance to the Trust Bank. Some young guy shot me. In the right shoulder, I think."

The nurse flashed a nervous smile in his direction. "I'm sorry, Mr. Katagiri, but you haven't been shot."

"I haven't? Are you sure?"

"As sure as I am that there was no earthquake this morning."

Katagiri was stunned. "Then what the hell am I doing in a hospital?"

"Somebody found you lying in the street, unconscious. In the Kabukicho neighborhood of Shinjuku. You didn't have any external wounds. You were just out cold. And we still haven't figured out why. The doctor's going to be here soon. You'd better talk to him."

Lying in the street unconscious? Katagiri was sure he had seen the pistol go off, aimed at him. He took a deep breath and tried to get his head straight. He would start by putting all the facts in order.

"What you're telling me is, I've been lying in this hospital bed, unconscious, since early evening yesterday, is that right?"

"Right," the nurse said. "And you had a really bad night, Mr. Katagiri. You must have had some awful nightmares. I heard you yelling, 'Frog! Hey, Frog!' You did it a lot. You have a friend nicknamed Frog?"

Katagiri closed his eyes and listened to the slow, rhythmic beating of his heart as it ticked off the minutes of his life. How much of what he remembered had actually happened and how much was hallucination? Did Frog really exist, and had Frog fought with Worm to put a stop to the earthquake? Or had that just been part of a long dream? Katagiri had no idea what was true anymore.

⊙ ⊙ ⊙ ⊙ ⊙ ⊙ ⊙ ⊙

Frog came to his hospital room that night. Katagiri awoke to find him in the dim light, sitting on a steel folding chair, his back against the wall. Frog's big, bulging eyelids were closed in straight slits.

"Frog," Katagiri called out to him.

Frog slowly opened his eyes. His big white stomach swelled and shrank with his breathing. "I meant to meet you in the boiler room at night the way I promised," Katagiri said, "but I had an accident in the evening—something totally unexpected—and they brought me here."

Frog gave his head a slight shake. "I know. It's OK. Don't worry. You were a great help to me in my fight, Mr. Katagiri."

"I was?"

"Yes, you were. You did a great job in your dreams. That's what made it possible for me to fight Worm to the finish. I have you to thank for my victory."

"I don't get it," Katagiri said. "I was unconscious the whole time. They were feeding me intravenously. I don't remember doing anything in my dream."

"That's fine, Mr. Katagiri. It's better that you don't remember. The whole terrible fight occurred in the area of imagination. That is the precise location of our battlefield. It is there that we experience our victories and our defeats. Each and every one of us is a being of limited duration: All of us eventually go down to defeat.

But as Ernest Hemingway saw so clearly, the ultimate value of our lives is decided not by how we win but by how we lose. You and I together, Mr. Katagiri, were able to prevent the annihilation of Tokyo. We saved 150,000 people from the jaws of death. No one realizes it, but that is what we accomplished."

"How did we manage to defeat Worm? And what did I do?"

"We gave everything we had in a fight to the bitter end. We—" Frog snapped his mouth shut and took one great breath. "We used every weapon we could get our hands on, Mr. Katagiri. We used all the courage we could muster. Darkness was our enemy's ally. You brought in a foot-powered generator and used every ounce of your strength to fill the place with light. Worm tried to frighten you away with phantoms of the darkness, but you stood your ground. Darkness vied with light in a horrific battle, and in the light I grappled with the monstrous Worm. He coiled himself

around me and bathed me in his horrid slime. I tore him to shreds, but still he refused to die. All he did was divide into smaller pieces. And then..." Frog fell silent, but soon, as if dredging up his last ounce of strength, he began to speak again. "Fyodor Dostoevsky, with unparalleled tenderness, depicted those who have been forsaken by God. He discovered the precious quality of human existence in the ghastly paradox whereby men who have invented God were forsaken by that very God. Fighting with Worm in the darkness, I found myself thinking of Dostoevsky's 'White Nights.' I..." Frog's words seemed to founder. "Mr. Katagiri, do you mind if I take a brief nap? I am utterly exhausted."

"Please," Katagiri said. "Take a good, deep sleep."

"I was finally unable to defeat Worm," Frog said, closing his eyes. "I did manage to stop the earthquake, but I was only able to carry our battle to a draw. I inflicted injury on him, and he on me. But to tell you the truth, Mr. Katagiri..."

"What is it, Frog?"

"I am, indeed, pure Frog, but at the same time I am a thing that stands for a world of un-Frog."

"Hmm, I don't get that at all."

"Neither do I," Frog said, his eyes still closed. "It's just a

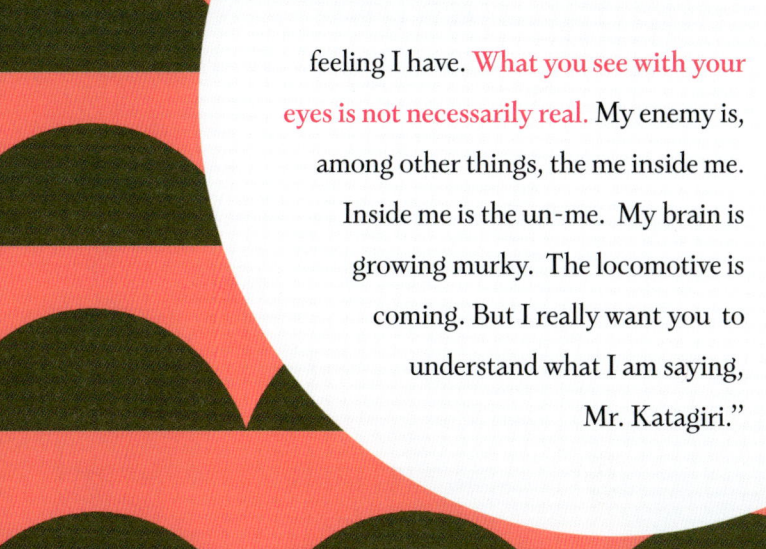

feeling I have. What you see with your eyes is not necessarily real. My enemy is, among other things, the me inside me. Inside me is the un-me. My brain is growing murky. The locomotive is coming. But I really want you to understand what I am saying, Mr. Katagiri."

目に見えるものが本当の
ものとはかぎりません。

"You're tired, Frog. Go to sleep. You'll get better."

"I am slowly returning to the murk, Mr. Katagiri. And yet...I..."

Frog lost his grasp on words and slipped into a coma. His arms hung down almost to the floor, and his big, wide mouth drooped open. Straining to focus his eyes, Katagiri was able to make out deep cuts covering Frog's entire body. Discolored streaks ran through his skin, and there was a sunken spot on his head where the flesh had been torn away.

Katagiri stared long and hard at Frog, who sat there now wrapped in the thick cloak of sleep. As soon as I get out of this hospital, he thought, I'll buy *Anna Karenina* and "White Nights" and read them both. Then I'll have a nice, long literary discussion about them with Frog.

Before long, Frog began to twitch all over. Katagiri assumed at first that these were just normal involuntary movements in sleep, but he soon realized his mistake. There was something unnatural about the way Frog's body went on jerking, like a big doll being shaken by someone from behind. Katagiri held his breath and watched. He wanted to run over to Frog, but his own body remained paralyzed.

  After a while, a big lump formed over Frog's right eye. The same kind of huge, ugly boil broke out on Frog's shoulder and side and then over his whole body. Katagiri could not imagine what was happening to Frog. He stared at the spectacle, barely breathing.

Then, all of a sudden, one of the boils burst with a loud pop. The skin flew off, and a sticky liquid oozed out, sending a horrible smell across the room. The rest of the boils started popping, one after another, twenty or thirty in all, flinging skin and fluid onto the walls. The sickening, unbearable smell filled the hospital room. Big black holes were left on Frog's body

where the boils had burst, and wriggling, maggot-like worms of all shapes and sizes came crawling out. Puffy white maggots. After them emerged some kind of small, centipede-like creatures, whose hundreds of legs made a creepy rustling sound. An endless stream of these things came crawling out of the holes. Frog's body—or the thing that had once been Frog's body—was totally covered by these creatures of the night.

His two big eyeballs fell from their sockets onto the floor, where they were devoured by black bugs with strong jaws.

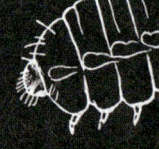

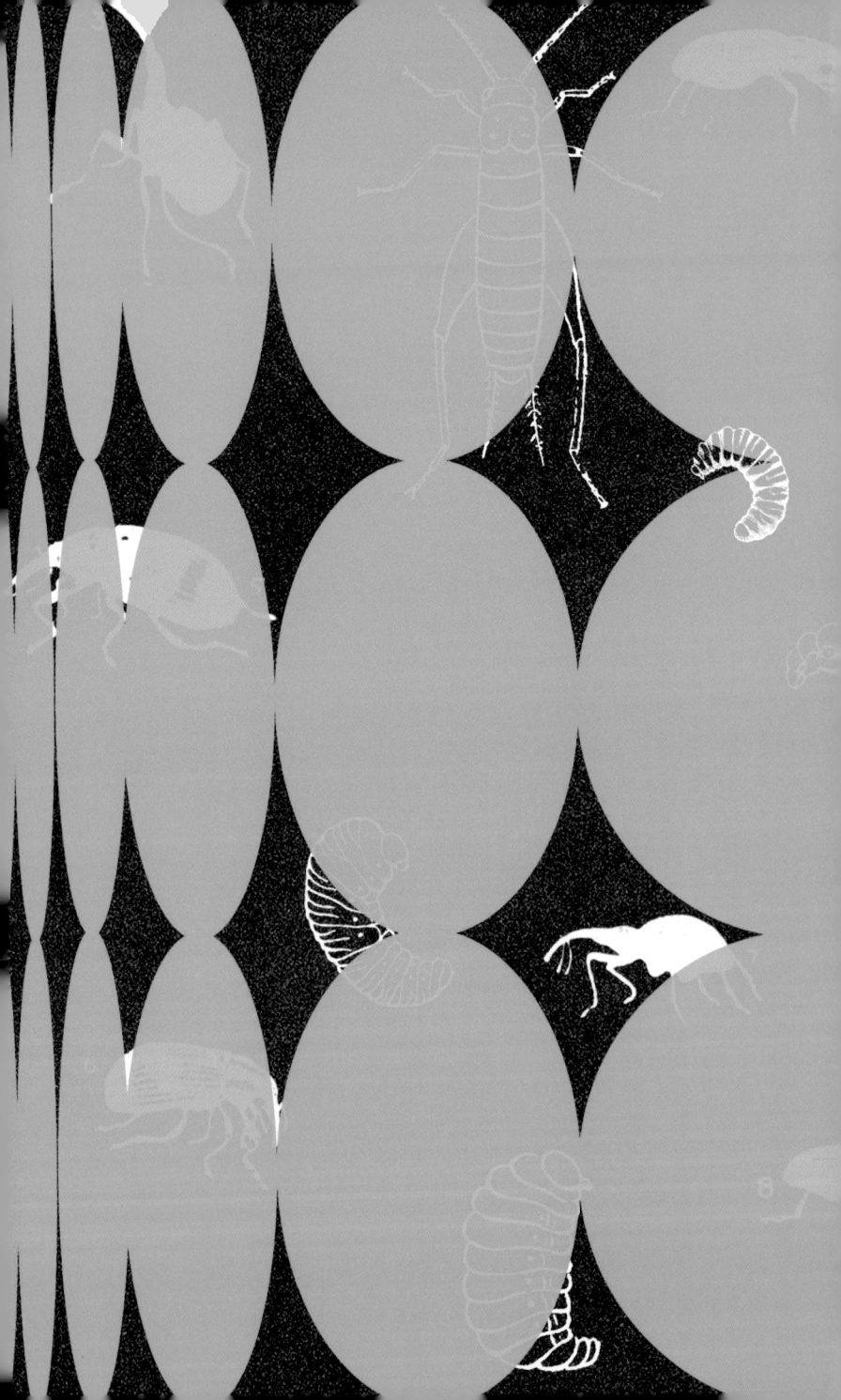

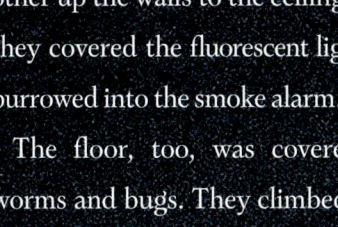

Crowds of slimy worms raced each other up the walls to the ceiling, where they covered the fluorescent lights and burrowed into the smoke alarm.

The floor, too, was covered with worms and bugs. They climbed up the lamp and blocked the light, and, of course, they crept onto Katagiri's bed. Hundreds of them came burrowing under the covers. They crawled up his legs, under his bed gown, between his thighs. The smallest worms and maggots crawled inside his anus and ears and nostrils. Centipedes pried open his mouth and crawled inside, one after another. Filled with an intense despair, Katagiri screamed.

Someone snapped a switch and light filled the room.

"Mr. Katagiri!" called the nurse. Katagiri opened his eyes to the light. His body was soaked in sweat. The bugs were gone. All they had left behind in him was a horrible, slimy sensation.

"Another bad dream, eh? Poor dear." With quick, efficient movements, the nurse readied an injection and stabbed the needle into his arm.

He took a long, deep breath and let it out. His heart was expanding and contracting violently.

"What were you dreaming about?"

Katagiri was having trouble differentiating dream from reality. "What you see with your eyes is not necessarily real," he told himself aloud.

"That's so true," the nurse said with a smile. "Especially where those dreams are concerned."

"Frog," he murmured.

"Did something happen to Frog?" she asked.

"He saved Tokyo from being destroyed by an earthquake. All by himself."

"That's nice," the nurse said, replacing his near-empty intravenous-feeding bottle with a new one. "We don't need any more awful things happening in Tokyo. We have plenty already."

"But it cost him his life. He's gone. I think he went back to the murk. He'll never come here again."

Smiling, the nurse toweled the sweat from his forehead. "You were very fond of Frog, weren't you, Katagiri?"

"Locomotive," Katagiri mumbled. "More than anybody." Then he closed his eyes and sank into a restful, dreamless sleep.

In 1978, Haruki Murakami was twenty-nine and running a jazz bar in downtown Tokyo. One April day, the impulse to write a novel came to him suddenly while watching a baseball game. That first novel, *Hear the Wind Sing*, won a new writers' award and was published the following year. More followed, including *A Wild Sheep Chase* and *Hard-Boiled Wonderland and the End of the World*, but it was *Norwegian Wood*, published in 1987, that turned Murakami from a writer into a phenomenon.

In works such as *The Wind-Up Bird Chronicle, 1Q84, What I Talk About When I Talk About Running, Men Without Women* and *The City and Its Uncertain Walls* Murakami's distinctive blend of the mysterious and the everyday, of melancholy and humour, continues to enchant readers, ensuring his place as one of the world's most acclaimed and well-loved writers. "Super-Frog Saves Tokyo" is one of Murakami's most iconic stories and was first published in English in Jay Rubin's translation in the collection *after the quake* in 2002. Murakami first published *after the quake* in Japan in 2000 in response to the devastating Kobe earthquake of 1995.

Picture Acknowlegements

Illustrations © Seb Agresti: pp. 2-3, 6-7, 8-9, 24-25, 26-27, 34-35, 36-37, 44-45, 60-61, 66-67

Illustrations © Suzanne Dean: pp. 4-5, 10-11, 12-13, 16-17, 18-19, 20-21, 22-23, 28-29, 30-31, 32-33, 38-39, 40-41, 46-47, 48-49, 52-53, 54-55, 58-59, 64-65, 68-69, 70-71, 72-73, 76-77, 78-79, 82-83, 88-89

Illustrations © Seb Agresti and Suzanne Dean: pp. i-1, 14-15, 42-43, 50-51, 56-57, 62-63, 74-75, 80-81, 84-85, 86-87

Alamy: Joseph Conrad p. 48, *Anna Karenina* book cover pp. 54, 75

Mary Evans: Ernest Hemingway p. 71

Shutterstock: Friedrich Nietzsche p. 41, graphic elements pp. 10-11, 20-21, 22-23, 50-51, 89-90

The London Library: insects sourced from old books: pp. 80-81, 82-83

Seb Agresti is a professional illustrator who has lived and worked in Japan and has been an avid reader of Murakami's works for many years. His illustrations have been featured in renowned publications such as the *New Yorker*, the *New York Times*, and *The Economist*, as well as on murals, record covers, and book covers.

Designed and illustrated by Vintage Creative Director Suzanne Dean.